Estela

and her CHRISTMAS SANDWICH CATASTROPHE

R. Aspen York

Illustrated by Sergio De Giorgi

AuthorHouse™
1663 Liberty Drive
Bloomington, IN 47403
www.authorhouse.com
Phone: 1 (800) 839-8640

Published by AuthorHouse 02/17/2016

ISBN: 978-1-5049-7559-9 (sc)
ISBN: 978-1-5049-7983-2 (hc)
ISBN: 978-1-5049-7560-5 (e)

Library of Congress Control Number: 2016902532

Print information available on the last page.

Any people depicted in stock imagery provided by Thinkstock are models,
and such images are being used for illustrative purposes only.
Certain stock imagery © Thinkstock.

This book is printed on acid-free paper.

Because of the dynamic nature of the Internet, any web addresses or links contained in this book may have changed
since publication and may no longer be valid. The views expressed in this work are solely those of the author and do not
necessarily reflect the views of the publisher, and the publisher hereby disclaims any responsibility for them.

authorHOUSE®

Estela and her Christmas Sandwich Catastrophe

It was the Christmas season in the uber-hip Moose Town, New York. Estela walked down Midtown Moohattan with her stylish hat protecting her beautiful golden m-shaped curls. Her eyes were opened wide as she admired all the countless lights, beautiful holiday decorations and window displays.

4

Estela stood tall beside the beautifully decorated Rockefeller Center Christmas tree. The tree was decorated with old fashion tin cans, red berries, lights and paper garlands. The residents of Moohattan appreciated the construction workers putting up the Rockefeller Center Christmas tree during the Great Depression in celebration of their early completion of the Rockefeller Center.

Estela stomach started to growl really loud as she continued to watch the construction workers celebrate their success. She sipped on her hot chocolate, munched on her biscuits and then reached her hand into her bag in search of more food.

Her face frowned as she pulled out the sandwich that her mother made for her. Estela appreciated the wholesome sandwich that her mom made for her as it was filled with lots of love, but she disliked sandwiches as she found them boring to eat. Why can't a sandwich be as merry as Christmas Estela thought to herself?

MOOSE
HUGS....!!
LOVE
MAMMA MO

Estela opened her gourmet sandwich. Her sandwich was packed with cranberry sauce, mayo, lettuce and brie. The sandwich was full of flavour, but was not appealing for Estela to eat.

Her stomach continued to growl louder and louder.

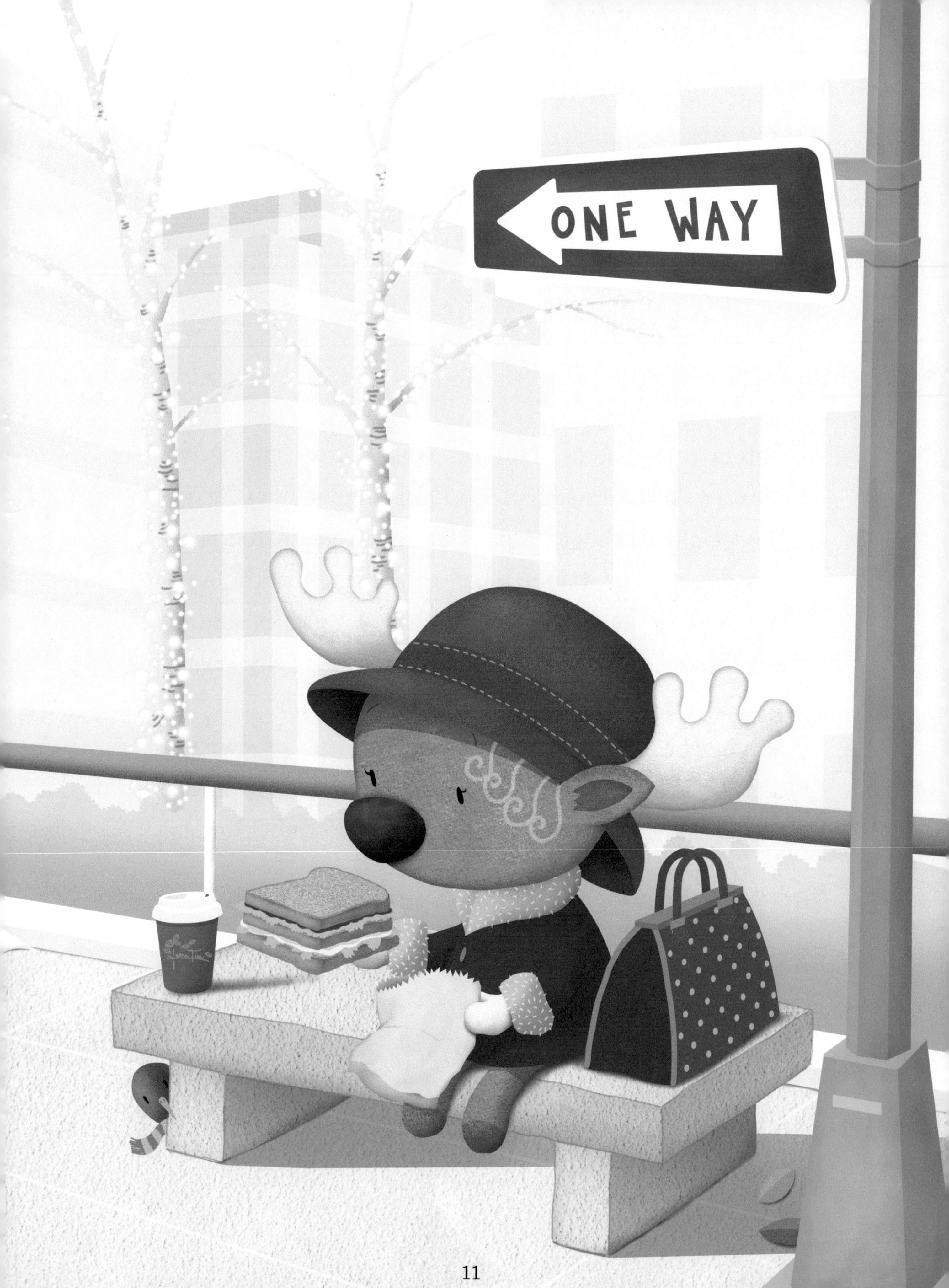
ONE WAY

Estela remembers when she was a mini moose her mom was the queen of making sandwiches for all the neighborhood moose. Her mom would dress up the double and triple layer sandwiches with fancy toppings or keep the sandwiches simple by adding her famous homemade peanut butter and jelly spread to the sandwiches. She would also then cut her sandwiches diagonal before serving the sandwiches to the neighborhood moose. The neighborhood moose would describe her mom sandwiches as the President Moo Obama's speech of all sandwiches.

"Sandwiches are your best friends as they give you energy to walk, shop, study and sing all day. Sandwiches are your best friends", sang a couple of construction workers with a karaoke-voice on Fifth Avenue.

Estela continued to watch her sandwich as the construction workers continued to sing. She started to recall another awful childhood sandwich memory.

Estela remembers when she was a mini moo she would hide her sandwiches underneath the family couch in the living room in hopes that nobody would find her sandwiches. Her plan was a success until her parents had company over and the company's dog would soon after sniff then pull the stale sandwiches from underneath the couch. Estela blushed as she remembers the extent she went through when she was a child to hide her sandwiches.

It is true thought Estela — sandwiches do give you energy, but are everyone best friend except for mine.

All of a sudden an ornament shaped into a heart fell down from the Rockefeller Center Christmas tree into the palm of Estela's hand.

Estela looked at the ornament and had an idea. She bent down and placed her sandwich on her bag and used the heart shaped ornament to press into her sandwich to produce the shape of a heart.

She then took a big bite into her heart shaped sandwich and smiled. A nearby sparrow flew and landed next to Estela. The sparrow grabbed the other half of her heart shaped sandwich and started singing the construction workers beautiful karaoke song – "Sandwiches are your best friends as they give you energy to walk, shop, study and sing all day. Sandwiches are your best friends".

Estela gave the sparrow a big hug and then looked up at the Rockefeller Christmas tree and thanked the tree for helping adding a little more merry to Estela's sandwich.

Printed in the United States
By Bookmasters